PUFFIN BOOKS

Eric's Elephant
on Holiday

Other titles in the First Young Puffin series

Eric's Elephant on Holiday

John Gatehouse

Illustrated by
Sue Cony

PUFFIN BOOKS

In memory of
Joice Gatehouse
and for Emma and Wendy

PUFFIN BOOKS

Published by the Penguin Group
Penguin Books Ltd, 27 Wrights Lane, London W8 5TZ, England
Penguin Books USA Inc., 375 Hudson Street, New York, New York 10014, USA
Penguin Books Australia Ltd, Ringwood, Victoria, Australia
Penguin Books Canada Ltd, 10 Alcorn Avenue, Toronto, Ontario, Canada M4V 3B2
Penguin Books (NZ) Ltd, 182–190 Wairau Road, Auckland 10, New Zealand

Penguin Books Ltd, Registered Offices: Harmondsworth, Middlesex, England

First published by Hamish Hamilton Ltd 1995
Published in Puffin Books 1997
1 3 5 7 9 10 8 6 4 2

Text copyright © John Gatehouse, 1995
Illustrations copyright © Sue Cony, 1995
All rights reserved

The moral right of the author and illustrator has been asserted

Filmset in Plantin

Made and printed in Hong Kong by Imago Publishing Limited

Eric owned a very unusual pet.

It was a real, live, white elephant that Eric had won at the Church Jumble Sale.

Eric's elephant followed him everywhere.

Well, almost everywhere.

"We're going on holiday in our caravan tomorrow," Eric's mum said, one summer's day.

"Yippee!" cheered Eric. "I love holidays."

"TOOT! TOOT!" trumpeted Eric's elephant, feeling just as excited. She had never been on holiday before.

Eric's dad shook his head. "Sorry, Eric," he said, firmly. "Your elephant can't go. She's too big!"

Eric's elephant tried to squeeze into the
caravan. But it was no use. Only her trunk
could fit through the door.

"You'll have to take her to the animal
sanctuary until we return," said Eric's
mum.

"But she'll be lonely," said Eric. "And she's very useful. Really she is!"

Eric's mum was too busy trying to close her bulging suitcase to answer.

"Let my elephant do that," said Eric, pushing his elephant through the front door.

Eric's elephant sat down on the suitcase. The lid snapped shut.

"See?" said Eric, proudly. "She really is useful!"

Eric's elephant was very heavy though. The suitcase couldn't hold her weight. It collapsed in pieces beneath her.

FLUMMMPH!

"My suitcase – it's ruined!" yelled Eric's mum, dancing up and down, and feeling very cross. "GET YOUR ELEPHANT OUT OF THE HOUSE!"

Eric pushed his elephant back out through the front door.

"Mum's going bonkers again," sighed Eric, leading his elephant down the street. "I'd better take you to the animal sanctuary, after all."

Eric's elephant felt very sad. She didn't want Eric to leave her. And she didn't want to miss the holiday.

The woman at the animal sanctuary didn't want Eric to leave his elephant with her, either.

"I don't mind cats and dogs," she said, glaring at Eric's elephant. "And gerbils are quite nice. But an elephant is a different kettle of fish."

"She's not a fish," said Eric. "She's an elephant!"

Eric's elephant didn't like the animal sanctuary. The other animals made her nervous.

A big dog in a cage barked loudly.
"WOOF!"

Eric's elephant leapt back in fright, and
knocked over a whole row of cages.

CRRAAASSSSH!

All the animals rushed madly about the
yard.

"GET THAT MONSTER OUT OF
HERE!" bellowed the woman, who was
struggling to stop a hamster from running
up her skirt.

Eric took his elephant back home again.

"Mum will go even more bonkers when I
tell her what's happened," he sighed.

Eric's dad was going slightly bonkers,
too.

"The car won't start," he grumbled. "We won't be able to go on holiday. We'll have to stay at home," he moaned.

"I've got an idea," said Eric. "We can let my elephant pull the caravan! Then she can go on holiday, too!"

"Well . . . I'm not sure," said Eric's dad.

"I am," said Eric's mum. "We're going. And we're taking Eric's elephant with us."

"Yippee!" cheered Eric.

"TOOT! TOOT!" trumpeted his elephant.

The next morning, Eric's dad fixed a harness to the elephant so she could pull the caravan. Eric sat on her back, to make sure she went the right way.

They arrived at the caravan park after lunch. Once they had unharnessed the elephant they all hurried down to the beach.

"I love the seaside," said Eric, running across the hot sand in his bare feet.

He could see lots of people with their buckets and spades and water-wings.

Mr Sprout and Mrs Groggins were
sunbathing on the beach. P.C. Crumble was
paddling in the water.

"Oh no," groaned Mr Sprout, when he
saw Eric's elephant. "If I had known she
was coming, I'd have gone to Bognor
instead."

Mr Sprout had had trouble with Eric's
elephant before. So had P.C. Crumble and
Mrs Groggins.

Eric led his elephant on to the beach.

"Now try and behave," Eric said. "We don't want to get into any trouble."

Eric's elephant wasn't listening. She had seen a group of children playing with a big, bouncy beach-ball.

"Hey! Come back!" cried Eric, as his elephant chased after it.

The elephant pounded along the beach, knocking over sandcastles and trampling on picnics. She tried to catch the beach-ball with her trunk.

"Look out!" cried Eric, as she tripped over her own feet and accidentally fell on the beach-ball. It burst with a loud BANG!

"TOOT!" trumpeted Eric's elephant,
looking surprised.

The children were very cross.

"Go away!" they shouted. "We don't
want you here!"

"I told you to behave," groaned Eric.
"Now everyone is going bonkers!"

Eric's elephant wasn't listening. She was
too busy leaping into the water to cool off.

SPLOOOOSSSSH! She created a big
wave that splashed cold water all over Mr
Sprout and Mrs Groggins. Then she
squirted water at P.C. Crumble, and
knocked off his hat.

"I'm beginning to wish I had never brought you on holiday," sighed Eric, as Mr Sprout, Mrs Groggins and P.C. Crumble went off to complain to Eric's dad.

Suddenly, Eric heard a loud cry.
"HELP!"
It came from a little boy who had been playing in the water. He had swum out too far, and was now too tired to swim back to the beach.

"Oh no!" Eric gasped. "He's in trouble! What are we going to do?"

Eric's elephant wasn't listening. She had already leapt back into the water with another big SPLOOOOSSSSH! She quickly swam over to the little boy and lifted him on to her back with her trunk.

Eric's elephant slowly returned to the
beach. A crowd had gathered and they all
clapped and cheered.

"You're a hero!" said Eric, proudly, as
his elephant handed the little boy back to
his mother.

All the children wanted to play with Eric and his elephant now. They had a silly game of water fights – Eric's elephant won. She had no trouble squirting *everyone*!

Then she let the children slide down her trunk into the water. She was having lots of fun!

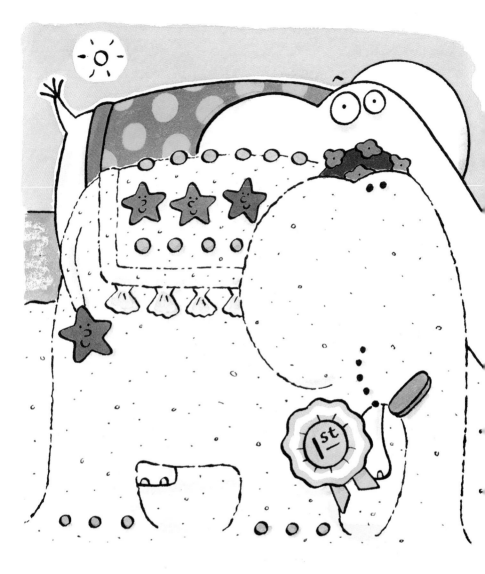

Eric and his elephant entered a
sandcastle-building competition. They built
a model of a sand-elephant, and won
FIRST PRIZE!

Eric shared his prize – a big basket of food – with everyone on the beach. Eric's elephant ate three times as much as anyone else.

"This is my best holiday ever!" said Eric.
"I'm so glad you came with us!"

"TOOT! TOOT!" agreed Eric's
elephant. She couldn't wait to go on her
NEXT holiday!